The Black Hen

or The Underground Inhabitants

By Antony Pogorelsky
Retold by Morse Hamilton
Illustrated by Tatyana Yuditskaya

COBBLEHILL BOOKS
Dutton • New York

To Galina Ficken, teacher and friend
—M.H.

To my daughter, Sofia
—T.Y.

A NOTE ABOUT THE AUTHOR

Antony Pogorelsky was the pen name of Aleksei Alekseevich Perovsky (1787–1836). As a young man, he took part in the defense of Russia against Napoleon's invading army. As a writer, he was known as "the Russian E.T.A. Hoffmann." Like the German romantic author, whose tale of the Mouse-King served as the basis for Tchaikovsky's ballet, *The Nutcracker*, and whose stories became the opera, *Tales of Hoffmann*, Pogorelsky used realistic detail to evoke an enchanted world.

Pogorelsky published a collection of romantic novellas, short stories, and a novel, *The Convent Girl*, an early example of Russian realism. The story of the magical black hen, written in 1829, is his best-known work and has long been a favorite in Russia.

Leo Tolstoy was asked once to name the books that had made the greatest impression on him as a child. Among half a dozen titles, he listed *The Black Hen* and, beside it, added "very great."

Text copyright © 1994 by Morse Hamilton
Illustrations copyright © 1994 by Tatyana Yuditskaya

Library of Congress Cataloging-in-Publication Data
Hamilton, Morse.
The black hen, or, The underground inhabitants / by Antony Pogorelsky ; retold by Morse Hamilton ; illustrated by Tatyana Yuditskaya.
    p.   cm.
Translation of: Chërnaia kuritsa, ili, Podzemnye zhiteli.
Summary: Alyosha follows a magical black hen down into an underground kingdom of little people and receives a special gift from their king.
    ISBN 0-525-65133-0
[1. Fairy tales.]   I. Yuditskaya, Tatyana, ill.
II. Pogorel 'skiĭ, Antoniĭ, 1787–1836. Chërnaia kuritsa, ili, Podzemnye zhiteli.   III. Title.
PZ8.H175B1   1994   92-28599
[Fic]—dc20   CIP   AC

Published in the United States by Cobblehill Books, an affiliate of Dutton Children's Books, a division of Penguin Books USA Inc.
375 Hudson Street, New York, New York 10014

Designed by Sylvia Frezzolini
Printed in Hong Kong
First Edition   10 9 8 7 6 5 4 3 2 1

*L*ong ago, when St. Petersburg was the capital of all Russia, there was in that city a famous boarding school. During the week the boys ate their meals and slept at the school, but when Saturday came, they went home to their families. All except Alyosha, whose parents lived a journey of several days from the capital. On weekends and holidays, the same building that had rung with talk and laughter suddenly seemed large and empty.

So Alyosha learned to entertain himself. If the weather was cold and wet, as it often is in a city so far north, he spent hours reading. His favorite books were about the old days, when there was still magic in the world.

If the weather was nice, he was allowed to play in the school yard. He liked to feed bread crumbs to the chickens that were kept there. His favorite was a black hen with a tuft of feathers on her head. "Blacky" always came when he called her and even let him stroke her.

One day when Alyosha was in the yard, the back door opened, and the cook came out with a knife in her hand. "Alyosha!" she shouted. "Help me catch one of these hens!"

So that is why the hens keep disappearing, the boy thought.

The cook started running back and forth in the snow, calling, "Here, nice chicky-chick!" Under her breath, she added, "Just wait till I catch one of you scrawny little beasts."

Alyosha's heart went thump, thump. His favorite, the black hen, seemed to be crying out to him:

> *Cackle, cackle, cack!*
> *Alyosha, save Blacky!*
> *Cackle, cack, cacky,*
> *It's me, Bla—!*

The cook had seized the hen by the tail feathers.

With a loud sob, Alyosha threw himself at the cook. "Please," he cried, "don't kill her."

The woman was so startled she let go of the hen, who flew up onto the roof of a nearby shed.

"Nice cook!" Alyosha pleaded. "Please let Blacky live. I'll give you a present if you promise not to hurt her."

He reached in his pocket and took out an *imperial*, a gold coin, which his grandmother had given him. The cook snatched up the coin and hurried back into the house.

Blacky flew down from the roof. All morning she followed Alyosha around the yard, beating her wings and clucking. It was as if she knew he had saved her life.

Alyosha went to bed early that night. He was all alone in the dormitory. As he lay on his side, staring dreamily at the empty bed next to his, its long top sheet seemed to billow, there was a scratching sound, and a voice whispered his name.

Alyosha rubbed his eyes. Sure enough, the sheet really bulged. "Alyosha!" the voice said again. The sheet lifted, and out stepped—the black hen.

"Oh, it's you!" said Alyosha, sitting up and clapping his hands. "How did you get in here?"

The black hen shook her wings and flew up next to him. "Yes, it's me," she said in a human voice. "You're not afraid, are you?"

"I'm not afraid of you. I love you," Alyosha said.

"Then get dressed quickly and come with me. I have something to show you."

Alyosha laughed. "How am I supposed to get dressed in the dark?"

The black hen flapped her wings and all about the room—on the floor, on the dresser, even on the washbasin—little candles in silver candle holders appeared.

Alyosha climbed out of bed and put on his clothes. The black hen flapped her wings again. This time, the candles disappeared, and the bedroom door opened by itself.

"Come," whispered the hen. "No talking. And don't touch anything."

Alyosha followed her out into the hall-
way, across the school lobby, and into a pri-
vate apartment belonging to two old ladies.
The ladies themselves were asleep in their
narrow beds. Nearby was a cockatoo in
a golden cage. Next to the beds was a sly
gray cat, carefully washing itself and eye-
ing them.

Just as Alyosha was passing, the cat held
out its paw and, without thinking, the boy
took it. At once the parrot started screech-
ing, "Idiot! Idiot!" and the two old ladies
sat up in bed. Alyosha ran to catch up with
the black hen, who had already disappeared
into the next room.

"Now look what you've done," muttered
the hen, pushing the door shut behind
them. "You have awakened the knights."

"The knights?" said Alyosha. "What
knights?"

"You shall see."

She led Alyosha down a staircase into
what looked like an ordinary cellar, except
that there were corridors and corridors,
some of them so narrow and low that Alyosha had to stoop over to pass through
them. At last they came to a large, win-
dowless room, lit by three chandeliers. On
two of the walls knights in glittering armor
and plumed helmets were suspended. They
held spears and shields in their iron hands.

The black hen tiptoed by them as quietly
as she could. Alyosha tried to do the same,
but just as they reached the brass door on
the other side, the knights leapt from the
walls and began to hurl their spears at
the hen.

The black hen shook her comb and flapped her wings and started to grow. She grew and grew until she was taller than the knights. Then they went at each other, tooth and claw. Alyosha was terrified. The room tilted and seemed to grow dark, and he tumbled to the floor.

When next he opened his eyes, Alyosha was in his own bed and it was morning. He longed to go outside, to make sure the black hen was safe, but all that day a snowstorm raged.

That night he went to bed early and waited in the dark. As he had hoped, the sheet moved, then lifted, and again out stepped the black hen.

"You're all right!" he cried.

"No thanks to you. Last night I told you not to touch anything, but what did you do? You touched the cat, who woke up the parrot, who woke the old ladies, who woke up the knights that guard the brass door. I'm lucky to be alive."

"Sorry," said Alyosha, hanging his head.

"Well, follow me again tonight. But this time do as you are told."

"I will," said Alyosha, jumping out of bed. "I promise."

Everything happened as it had the night before. The little candles appeared and disappeared, the door to the dormitory opened by itself. Again they walked through the lobby and into the old ladies' apartment, where the parrot slept in its golden cage and the cat sat, washing its paw.

This time Alyosha held his hands behind his back, so he would not be tempted to touch anything, and the old ladies slept on undisturbed.

Alyosha and the hen got safely past the knights. Tonight the brass door opened. Beyond lay a magnificent hall, at one end of which stood a miniature throne, all of gold.

"Wait for me here," said the black hen. "I won't be long."

It was like being in a royal palace, except that the ceiling was so low that Alyosha could touch it with his hand. As he was admiring the marble walls, a side door opened, and little people not nearly as tall as he was began streaming in. They chattered in a strange language, until the great doors at the end of the hall were thrown wide. All talking ceased. The little men removed their hats and arrayed themselves before the throne. In strode another little man with a crown on his head.

Guessing that this must be the king, Alyosha made a deep bow. The king inclined his head in a friendly way and beckoned for the boy to approach the throne.

"Alyosha," he said. "We have long known what a good boy you are. And that is why we decided to trust you with the secret of our existence.

It is useful to have allies. Then the day before yesterday you proved your worthiness when you saved the life of our chief minister."

"When I did what?"

"When you saved our minister's life."

One of the king's men stepped forward, and Alyosha took a good look at him. He was dressed all in black, except that on his head he wore a quaint hat, the color of raspberries, and jagged like a coxcomb. His smile looked familiar.

But Alyosha loved truth more than praise and could not take credit for something he had not done. "Your majesty," he said, "there must be some mistake. The day before yesterday I saved a hen. I think cook wanted to kill it because it never lays any eggs."

"What!" cried the king. "Our chief minister is no hen!"

Here the man dressed in black whispered something in the king's ear, and as he did so, Alyosha recognized him. It was Blacky—only now he was a court minister!

Alyosha started to beg his pardon, but the king held up his royal hand. "Since you have done us this great service, we wish to reward you. Tell us what you want, and if it is in our power to grant, we shall do so gladly."

"Don't be shy, Alyosha," prompted the chief minister, smiling.

Now if the boy had had more time to consider, no doubt he would have asked for something sensible. But as it was, he blurted out the first thought that came to his mind: "I wish I could memorize my lessons without having to study."

"I did not know that you were such a lazybones," said the king, frowning, "but no matter." He made a sign, and a page stepped forward, bearing a golden plate on which lay a single seed.

"As long as you keep this seed, your wish will come true," the king said. "But you must never tell a living soul what you have seen here tonight. If you do, you will lose our favor and also cause us great harm."

Alyosha wrapped the seed in a piece of tissue paper and put it in his pocket.

"Now," said the king, "before our honored guest returns to the world above, let him be refreshed and entertained."

So Alyosha was shown around the underground kingdom, and the marvels he saw there are beyond description. He was led down garden paths made of rubies, diamonds, and emeralds to a zoo in which underground creatures, such as moles and ferrets, were kept in tiny cages. After serving a snack of delicious desserts, Alyosha's hosts organized a royal hunt. The court groom led out the hobbyhorses.

"Be careful, sir," he said to Alyosha. "Yours has a will of his own."

The boy tried not to laugh, since a hobbyhorse is just a stick with a horse's head on one end, but no sooner had he straddled it, than it began to buck and start.

He held on tight, and off they galloped in pursuit of the rats and mice that threatened to overrun the underground kingdom.

Next morning the first thing Alyosha did when he woke up was to check his pocket. There in the piece of paper was the tiny seed that the little king had given him.

He did not have to wait very long to see if the seed really worked. Over winter break, the boys were supposed to memorize a long passage from their history book. Alyosha had not bothered to learn a single word. On the first day of classes, the headmaster called him to the front of the room. Alyosha touched his seed to give himself courage, opened his mouth—and rattled off the entire lesson.

Everyone was astounded. The next day, and the day after that, he repeated the performance. No matter what was assigned, Alyosha could recite it perfectly. This was unheard of. Parents from all over St. Petersburg came to see the child prodigy.

Naturally, the headmaster was very pleased, but he could not help noticing that a change had taken place in Alyosha. Since the boy did not have to learn his lessons, he played during study hours. His classmates, who had to do their work the old-fashioned way, began to resent him.

One day the headmaster said, "Alyosha, since you seem to have so much free time on your hands, I am assigning you twenty pages to learn by heart for tomorrow."

The man thought more work would sober the boy, but if you have a magic seed, twenty pages are no more difficult than two or three. Alyosha did not bother to open his book. He danced around the study hall like a monkey.

Next morning Alyosha swaggered to the front of the classroom, wearing a smile that seemed to say, I'm great and I know it. He opened his mouth . . . and nothing happened!

"We are waiting," said the headmaster, tapping his long fingers on the desk.

Alyosha's hand flew to his pocket, but the seed was gone—it must have fallen out. The boy was speechless.

"So," said the headmaster, "now you have decided to be stubborn. Well, I can be stubborn, too. Go to the dormitory and stay there until you have memorized all twenty pages."

Back in the dormitory, Alyosha got down on his hands and knees. He looked under the beds, lifting up people's shoes. The seed could be anywhere. What if he had lost it outside? He pictured one of the chickens coming across a nice, tasty seed. Peck . . .

"Oh, Blacky," he cried. "Where are you, now that I need you? Couldn't I have another seed?"

But no black hen flew to his aid. Instead, the door opened and the headmaster walked in.

"Have you memorized your lesson?" he asked.

Sadly the boy shook his head.

"In that case, you will stay here until you have. Here is your supper." He put a glass of water and a piece of bread down on the table next to Alyosha's bed and left.

Alyosha fetched his history book from the shelf where it had been gathering dust and began slowly to read the long assignment. Alas—he had grown so unused to studying that the words seemed to dance before his eyes.

When the other boys came in to get ready for bed, Alyosha approached one or two, but they turned away. For a long time he lay in the dark, remembering how everyone used to like him. Now he had no one—not even the black hen.

No sooner did he remember his friend
than the sheets hanging from the next bed
began to bulge, there was a familiar scratching sound, and the hen stepped out.

"Blacky!" said Alyosha in a loud whisper.
"I was afraid I would never see you again."

The black hen flew up beside him on the
bed. "I could never forget the boy who
saved my life," he said solemnly, "although
he bears little resemblance to the child I
see before me now."

Alyosha's eyes filled with tears. "Give me
another chance. I promise not to be so
selfish."

"I hope you mean that," said the hen,
seriously. All that night he stayed with the
boy, talking about the importance of being
modest and considerate. Finally, when the
first light of morning slipped through the
old shutters, he put something on Alyosha's
pillow. "Here, you dropped this in the yard.
Lucky for you *I* found it. Be good and remember your promise not to tell anyone
about us. Some people in the upper world
despise our magic. If they knew where we
lived, they would try to destroy us.
It's late. I must go now."

All the children were assembled in the classroom for the morning recitation. The headmaster asked Alyosha to step forward.

"So," he said, "have you learned your lesson?"

"Yes!" said Alyosha, and when he opened his mouth, twenty pages' worth of names and dates came pouring out. He could not resist looking around at the astonished faces of his classmates with a triumphant smirk.

"Well done," said the headmaster, his manner somewhat softened. "But tell me, why did you refuse to recite yesterday?"

"Because yesterday I did not know my lesson," Alyosha said truthfully.

"But when did you learn it?"

His voice quavering, Alyosha said, "This morning."

But his classmates shouted in chorus, "He's lying. He never once picked up his book."

Alyosha started to shake all over. What could he say to make the man believe him?

"The more gifted you are," the headmaster said sternly, "the more humble you should be. Yesterday you were obstinate; today it is obvious that you are lying. Somebody needs to teach you a lesson. Fetch me the birch rods."

Immediately, a servant was there with the rods.

Sobbing, Alyosha threw himself on the headmaster. "Please, sir, don't beat me!" he cried. "I promise I will mend my ways."

Seeing how frightened he looked, first one boy, then several, begged the headmaster not to beat him. "I will give you one more chance," the man said. "Only this time I expect the whole truth. Look at me, Alyosha. When did you memorize those twenty pages?"

Everyone was waiting. Alyosha lost his head completely and simply blurted out the whole story about the black hen, and the knights, and the little people underground. But the headmaster did not let him finish. "Dishonesty is not enough. Now you wish to make fools of us." He took up the rods . . .

It was after dark. Alyosha ached in body and heart. This time when he heard the familiar scratching sound and saw the sheet moving, he quickly turned the other way and shut his eyes. Someone tugged on his blanket. Alyosha peeked through his long eyelashes. The chief minister stood before him, dressed all in black.

"Alyosha," he said. "I can only stay a minute. I have come to say good-bye. Because you broke your word and told our secret, my people are packing. We must move tonight."

Alyosha could not speak. He reached out to take his friend's hand, but saw that his wrists were bound by tiny golden fetters. The boy let out a sob.

"If you wish to make amends, there is one thing you can do: Become again the kind boy who saved my life." He squeezed the boy's hand and stepped back under the sheet.

"Blacky," Alyosha called out after him, but Blacky was gone.

All night Alyosha lay awake. Just before dawn he heard noises underground. He got out of bed and put his ear to the floor. From deep under the room came the sounds of tiny horses clopping, wagons rumbling, people marching. Faintly he could hear the wails of women and children. Above the din one voice, grown dear to him, said over and over, "Good-bye, Alyosha. Good-bye."

Next morning the other boys found Alyosha lying on the floor, uncon-
scious. They called the headmaster, who called the doctor. For weeks,
Alyosha lay in a dangerous fever. When he finally began to recover,
everything that had happened seemed like a strange dream.

No one—neither the headmaster nor the other boys—ever referred to
the Black Hen or to Alyosha's punishment.

Alyosha became the modest, considerate boy he used to be, and everyone liked him again.

He studied his lessons and tried to be a model pupil. Of course, he
could no longer memorize twenty pages just like that. But then no one
ever asked him to.